USBORNE HOTSHOTS

CARD
TRICKS

USBORNE HOTSHOTS

CARD
TRICKS

Edited by Lisa Miles
Designed by Fiona Johnson

Photography by Howard Allman

Series editor: Judy Tatchell
Series designer: Ruth Russell

Based on material by Cheryl Evans,
Rebecca Heddle and Ian Keable-Elliott

CONTENTS

Getting started

Card tricks are fun to do and great to watch. All you need for the tricks in this book is one or two packs of cards, lots of time for practice – and an audience! Remember not to tell anyone how your tricks work. Magicians never reveal their secrets to anyone except fellow magicians.

Presentation

A successful card trick depends on presentation as well as technique. Your patter (what you say during the trick) should sound natural. Prepare what you are going to say and speak clearly, without rushing. Relax and stand naturally. Look directly at people as you talk to them, to make them feel part of the show. Vary short tricks with longer, more complex ones. Link different tricks smoothly and save your most spectacular one until last.

Choosing a pack of cards

Packs of cards come in different sizes. Choose one that feels comfortable in your hands. Packs with a white border around the back are best for tricks. This helps to disguise some moves as the edge of the card looks the same on both sides.

Left-handed?

In this book, the instructions for the tricks work best for right-handed people. If you are left-handed, you might want to reverse the instructions.

Misdirection

Misdirection is a way to hide secret moves – even when your audience is watching carefully. You use it to draw attention away from what you are doing. Lots of tricks use it.

For instance, to make people think something is in your left hand when it is in your right, watch your left hand and pay no attention to your right. Speaking also diverts attention because people look at your face as you talk.

Repeat a move casually a few times before you do a secret move. Then, people will not be watching your hands so closely.

Face-up or face-down?

The instructions in this book will tell you to deal either "face-up" or "face-down". Face-up means with the fronts showing, and face-down means with the backs showing.

Symbols

These symbols are used throughout this book to help explain the tricks.

The arrow shows you in which direction to move the cards.

The bubble shows you which card is being memorized, either by the magician or a volunteer.

Handling skills, shuffles and cuts

It is well worth getting used to these basic handling skills – they will help you to perform any type of card trick.

Overhand Shuffle

Shuffling disturbs the order of the pack. You can use this simple but effective shuffle in lots of tricks.

1. Rest the pack on a long edge in your left hand. Hold the short edges with your right fingers and thumb.

2. Press on the pack with your left thumb and lift your right hand. Your thumb will draw the top few cards down into your left hand.

3. Lift the pack over the drawn off cards and repeat steps 2 and 3, until all the cards are in your left hand.

Squaring the pack

When you need to neaten, or square, the pack, tap the edges on a table, or use your hands like this.

Cutting cards

Cutting the pack means dividing it and putting the bottom half on top. The order of the cards in each half does not change. When volunteers cut the pack as part of a trick, make sure they cut it like this.

1. Lift away around half of the cards from the top of the pack.

2. Put this half face-down on the table, next to the bottom half of the pack.

3. Put the bottom half face-down on top of the res of the pack.

Dealing the cards

You will often need to deal cards during a trick, so it's worth making sure that you can do it quickly and smoothly.

Rest the pack face-down on your left palm. Hold the long edges against your fingers, with your thumb resting on top. Using your thumb, slide the top card over a little. Take it in your right hand and lay it down on the table. Turn the card over to deal face-up.

Usually, when dealing to two people or more, you deal alternately, first to one, then the next and so on.

Classic Spread

Here is a way to spread the cards to offer to volunteers when you want them to choose one. This spread is called the Classic Spread. The cards will be in the same order when you close them again.

1. Hold the pack flat in one hand. Use your thumb to push cards off the top of the pack into your other hand a few at a time.

2. Spread the cards into a smooth fan shape. Support them with your fingers beneath and thumbs on top.

Try to make the edges of the fan look neat, like this.

Some easy tricks

The tricks on the next four pages are fairly easy, so try them to start off with.

Magic Sevens

For this trick, you need 21 cards, taken from the same pack.

Step 1

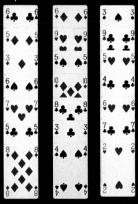

1. Lay three cards face-up in a row. Put a second card over each one, and so on until you have used them all. Ask someone to choose a card, but keep it secret.

2. Ask which line the chosen card is in. If it is in either of the end rows, pick up that row and move it into the middle. (You can collect the rows into three piles before doing this.)

3. Gather the three piles together, on top of one another, from left to right. Repeat Steps 1-3 twice more.

Step 2

Step 3

4. After you have gathered the cards for the last time, stack them face-down. From the top, count out ten cards. The eleventh is the chosen card.

8

Double Lift technique

With this technique, you seem to show the top card to your audience. In fact, you pick up the top two cards at once. Use your thumb to bend the top two cards slightly to lift them off as one. Hold the pack with a short edge toward your body, to obscure what you are doing.

It might help to bend this finger and press it against the cards.

Card Through Cards

1. This trick uses the Double Lift (see above). Double Lift the top two cards from a pack, holding them together so they look like one card. Let everyone see the card face.

2. Put the two cards down again on the top of the pack. Slide the top one off and put it at the bottom. Don't let anyone see its face, though.

After Step 2, the audience thinks the Ten of Spades is at the bottom.

3. Give the pack a sharp tap and say some magic words. Explain that this will bring the bottom card back to the top.

4. Pick off the top card and show that it is the same one that you showed in Step 1.

9

8 5 3 9 8 4 2 3 6 9 6 7 2 7 5 10 4 10 9 8 5 6 10 3 2 7 5 7 9 6 4 8 3 10 4 2 ♣ 2
♥ ♥ ◆ ♥ ◆ ♥ ◆ ♥ ◆ ♥ ◆ ♥ ♥ ◆ ◆ ♣ ♠ ♣ ◆ ♣ ♠ ♣ ♠ ♣ ♠ ♣ ♠ ♣ ♠ ◆ ♣ ♣ ◆ ♠ ◆

♠ ◆ ♠ ◆ ♠ ◆ ♠ ◆ ♠ ◆ ♠ ◆ ♠ ◆ ♣ ♥ ◆ ♥ ♣ ♥ ♣ ♥ ♣ ♥ ♣ ♥ ♥ ◆ ♥ ♥ ♣ ♥ ♣
8 5 ε 6 8 ♭ ε 9 6 9 ∠ 2 ∠ 5 ♭ 10 ♭ 01 6 8 ϛ 9 01 ε 2 ∠ 5 ∠ 6 9 ε 2 ♭ 8 ε 9 5 ε

1. Fan them out face-down in one hand. As someone to pick a card. Without making it obvious, point one half of the fan in their direction, so they take a card from that half. Keep the cards a little more closed up in the other half of the pack. Then close the fan.

2. Reopen the fan and ask them to put their card back. Move the fan around so that it goes in near the other end.

3. Close the fan and make a show of searching through the pack. No one else must see the cards. You should see the picked card easily — if it was red, it will be among the black cards, and if it was black, it will be with the reds.

Ask your volunteer whether this was the card he or she chose.

Rising Cards

In this trick, you put two cards into the middle of a pack and make them appear to rise magically to the top.

1. To prepare, put the Seven of Hearts and the Eight of Clubs face-down on top of the pack.

2. Take the Seven of Clubs and the Eight of Hearts from the pack, pretending to choose them at random. Show them briefly to the audience, without naming them.

3. Then put them into the middle of the pack.

4. Riffle (flick rapidly through) the edges of the pack with your fingers, saying this will cause the chosen cards to rise magically to the top of the pack.

5. Turn over the top two cards: the Seven of Hearts and the Eight of Clubs. These are not the cards you chose, but as you did not name them and they look very similar, your audience should not notice the difference.

These are the two cards which went on top of the pack, not the two in the middle.

11

The Glimpse

The Glimpse is a useful technique which allows you to know the bottom card of the pack. You can learn the Glimpse and some tricks which use it on the next four pages.

Glimpse technique

All you do is square the pack on the table, and glance at the card at the bottom as you do so. You can do this after shuffling, so that no one is suspicious.

Turn the pack slightly so you that can just about see the bottom card.

Card Search

1. Spread the cards into a fan. Ask someone to pick out a card and look at it without showing you.

2. Take half the pack in your right hand. Glimpse the bottom card and memorize it.

3. Ask your volunteer to put the card back on top of the cards in your left hand.

4. Put the cards from your right hand on top of them. Now the card chosen by the volunteer is the one under the Glimpsed card.

5. Turn the cards over. Explain that you are searching for the volunteer's card. Look for the Glimpsed card. The volunteer's card is on top of it.

Key Card Control

A control is a way of bringing a card to the top of the pack. You can use the Key Card Control to find a card and bring it up to the top of the pack.

1. Glimpse the bottom card.

2. Spread the pack face-down and ask someone to pick out a card without telling you what it is.

3. Cut the pack and lay the two halves on the table. Ask your volunteer to place their card on the top half, then complete the cut. Ask him to cut the pack a few times.*

The Glimpsed card stays with the chosen card.

4. Fan the cards face-up in your hands. Say "Your card is lost somewhere in here, isn't it?" as an excuse for looking through the pack for the Glimpsed card. The volunteer's chosen card is on top of it.

5. Take the chosen card and those to its right in one hand. Take the rest in the other.

6. Cut the half with the chosen card to the top, so that the chosen card is on top of the pack. Square the pack.

7. Ask your volunteer to take the top card. It is his chosen card.

See note on page 32.

Card spread on the table

Making a card spread, or fan, in your hands is shown on page 7. Here is a way to spread the cards on the table, instead of in your hands.

Lay the pack on the table. Touch the short edges of the pack with your fingers and thumb to square the pack.

Tap the left side of the cards with your first finger and sweep them to the right. With practice, the cards will make a long line.

Do As I Do

This trick needs two packs of cards.

1. Put the packs on a table. Ask someone to take one and copy you exactly.

2. Pick up your pack and start shuffling. Square the pack and do the Glimpse.

3. Then, ask your volunteer to swap packs with you.

4. Spread your pack on the table. Move your finger as if choosing a card then bring it down on a card. The volunteer copies you.

14

5. Tell the volunteer to memorize her chosen card. Pretend to memorize yours (you do not need to know it). Both of you put your chosen cards aside, face-down, then gather up your packs, keeping the cards in the same order.

6. Then, both cut your packs on the table. Put your chosen cards on the top halves of your packs before completing the cut. The trick will look more impressive if you cut the cards again.

7. Swap the packs again. Tell the volunteer to search through her new pack and find the card she memorized. Meanwhile, you search for the Glimpsed card, and take the one on top of it. Try to finish before the volunteer.

Ask her to lay her rd face-down on the ble. Put yours face-wn on top, forming X. Turn both over. ey are the same.

reveal the cards in an pressive way, flip them both er in one movement.

15

Magician's Choice

The technique

With Magician's Choice, you seem to let your volunteer choose freely, but in fact you manipulate what she says so that she "chooses" the card you want.

Ask your volunteer to point to a card.

1. In this example, you want the volunteer to choose the middle card. Ask her to point to a card. She might point to the middle one anyway.

2. If she points to the left or right one, say she has ruled out that card, and take it away. Repeat until she picks the card you want. Act confidently, and no one will question you.

Double Choice

1. Shuffle the pack and Glimpse the bottom card as you square the pack.

Glimpsed card

2. Make a fan or spread the cards out in a line. Ask a volunteer to take a card from the pack and memorize it without showing it to you.

3. Cut the pack and ask the volunteer to put her card on the top half. Complete the cut by putting the bottom half of the pack on top. Cut the pack a few times, saying you are losing her card.*

4. Look through the pack and pick out the Glimpsed card and the two cards on its right. Lay them down face-down in the same order. Tell her that you think one of them is her card.

5. Ask your volunteer to point to one of the three cards, and then use the technique of Magician's Choice to make her choose the middle card. This is the card she chose in Step 2.

6. As your volunteer turns over the middle card, thank her for choosing the same card twice.

*See note on page 32.

Shuffle Control

On this page is another way to bring a chosen card to the top. It is called the Shuffle Control. Instead of looking through the pack, you use a technique called In-jogging, which is explained below.

1. Ask someone to pick out a card and memorize it without showing you what it is.

2. Start an Overhand Shuffle. About halfway through, stop and ask the volunteer to place her card on top of the cards in your lower hand.

3. Now for the In-jogging. Shuffle a single card into your lower hand. Let it fall out of line so it sticks out a little in your direction.

4. Shuffle the rest of the cards. People will not see the in-jogged card.

5. Cut the cards below it to the top of the pack.

6. The chosen card is now on top.

18

Countdown Trick

This trick uses the Shuffle Control explained on the previous page.

1. Make a card spread and ask someone to pick a card. Use the Shuffle Control to bring it to the top. Ask the person to choose a number between five and ten.

2. Deal out that number of cards, face-down in a pile. Turn the last card, and say this is the chosen card. It is not, so look puzzled.

3. "Remember" that you did not say the magic words. Turn the card back over. Put the pile of dealt cards on the top of the pack. Say some magic words and tap the back of the pack.

4. Hand the pack to the volunteer and ask him to deal out the right number of cards. The last card dealt is the chosen card. This way the magic seems to happen in his hands, not yours.

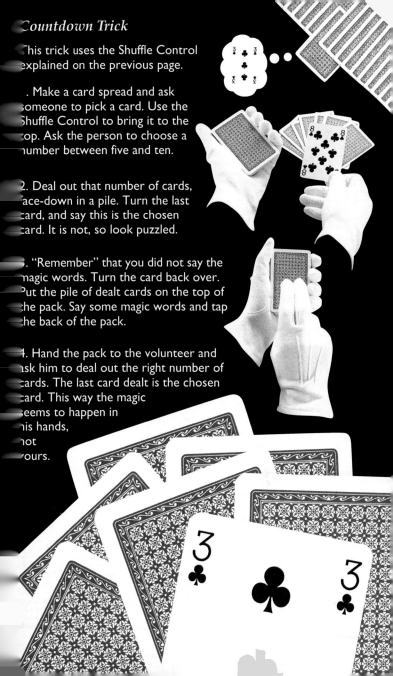

Challenge your audience

You can challenge your audience with the tricks on these two pages. Don't look too pleased when you make a fool of someone, though, or you might put your audience off.

Six in a Row

Lay out six cards so that you have three reds next to three blacks. Challenge a member of your audience to move the cards so that red and black cards alternate. They are allowed three moves, and each time can only pick up two cards, which must be next to each other. This is how to do it.

Red 1   Red 2   Red 3   Black 1   Black 2   Black 3

Start with the cards laid out like this.

---

1. Move Red 1 and Red 2 to the far right.

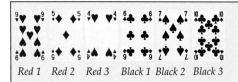

Red 3   Black 1   Black 2   Black 3   Red 1   Red 2

---

2. Move Black 3 and Red 1 to the far right.

 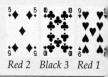

Red 3   Black 1   Black 2   Red 2   Black 3   Red 1

---

3. Move Red 3 and Black 1 into the space left by the last move.

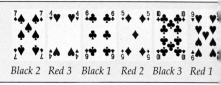

Black 2   Red 3   Black 1   Red 2   Black 3   Red 1

Three Card Trick

1. Lay three cards in a row, as shown here.

Card A   Card B   Card C

2. Ask a member of your audience which cards are farthest apart. Most people will say B and C. The answer, of course, is A and C.

Four in a Row

A

B

C

D   E   F

1. Make an L-shape with six cards, four down and three across. Ask a volunteer to move one card so that both rows have four cards in them.

B

C

E   F

2. When the volunteer looks puzzled, place card A on top of card D.

Catch It If You Can

Hold a card by the top corner. Ask a volunteer to position her hand halfway down the card, ready to catch it when you drop it.

Magician

Volunteer's hand must not be touching the card.

Bet her she cannot catch it before it hits the ground. Almost no one will be quick enough.

Your volunteer's reactions will get better with practice – so don't give her a second chance!

Mind-reading

With the tricks on these two pages, you can pretend to read someone else's mind. For the first trick, you will need a partner for some secret teamwork.

Pattern Codes

The volunteer points to one of the cards.

To do this trick, your partner lays out five cards in a row. You leave the room, and a volunteer chooses a card and points to it. When you come back in, your partner points to one of the other cards and asks, "Is it this one?" You answer "No", but the position in which she touches the card tells you where the chosen card is.

The secret is that you agree on a code, such as the one on the right. Each card has five positions. Your partner touches one of these positions, which tells you where the chosen card is. You can then answer by telling her which is the real chosen card.

Here, the partner is touching the top corner on her left, which means that the chosen card is fourth in the row.

Predictions

For this trick, you need two packs of cards. To prepare, Glimpse the bottom card of each pack in turn and use a Shuffle Control to bring them both to the top. The audience will think you are just shuffling.

1. Ask a volunteer to choose a pack. Remember the Glimpsed card for this pack. (You can forget the other Glimpsed card.) Ask the volunteer to deal five cards in a pile from the top of the pack.

2. Then ask her to lay them out in a row from left to right. Meanwhile, fan the other pack out and look at it. Ask the volunteer to look at her first card and say that you are going to read her mind.

3. Lay the card which matches the Glimpsed card from the volunteer's pack face-down, saying that you predict that this matches her first card. Ask her to tell the audience what it is and lay it face-down on top of yours.

4. Now you know what her first card is! Ask her to look at her second card. As she does so, lay down the card that matches her first one, pretending that this matches her second. Repeat this until all her cards have been laid. Her last card is the Glimpsed card.

5. Pick up the pile and take it behind your back. Take the first card and bring it to the back of the pile. Now reveal the matching pairs to your audience, by spreading them in a fan.

Sleight of hand

A sleight (say "slight") of hand is a secret move. Sleights let you perform tricks based on secret actions.

The Backslip

The Backslip is a fairly easy sleight, although it still needs practice. It is a way of cutting the cards to end up with the top card of the pack on top of the bottom half.

1. Hold the pack face-down in your left palm, with your thumb against one long edge and your fingers curled around the other edge.

2. Using your right fingers and thumb, take hold of the top half of the pack by the short edges. Lift the top half of the pack, as if you were opening a book.

3. Now lift off the top half of the pack completely, gripping the top card with your fingers to pull it onto the bottom half of the pack. Do this fairly quickly.

4. As you slide the top card off the pack, turn your left palm down to hide the move. If you do it all smoothly, no one should notice.

Turn your left wrist so that your palm hides the Backslip action.

Card Switch

1. Ask someone to think of a number between five and ten. Show her the top ten cards and ask her to memorize the card at her chosen number.

2. Now put the ten cards back on top of the pack, and split the pack doing a Backslip so that the top card goes onto the bottom half. Give your volunteer the top half of the pack, keeping the bottom half yourself.

Chosen card is sixth in pack.

3. Now ask her to tell you the number she chose and count that many cards, less one, back onto your half of the pack.

4. Say you will pick her card by cutting your half of the pack. Do a Backslip and bring the bottom section of cards to the top.

5. Ask her to turn her top card over, and turn your top card. Her chosen card is on your half of the pack.

25

Secret preparations

You will need a moment to prepare the pack for the tricks on these two pages. Be sure not to shuffle the pack by accident before you start to perform the trick.

Sixes and Sevens

1. Take all the sixes and sevens out of a pack of cards. Arrange the sixes and sevens like this. Show the cards to your audience.

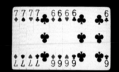

2. Ask a volunteer to cut the eight cards a few times. Most people do not know that this does not change the order of the cards. Take them back and say you can feel which ones are from which suit.

3. To prove it, take the eight cards behind your back. Hold them all in your right hand, the first four between your thumb and first finger, and the others between your first and second fingers.

4. With your left hand, take the top card of each set of four and lay them face-up on the table.

5. Repeat this with the remaining cards, each time taking the top card from each set. Take a while to make each pair. The trick will seem harder, and more impressive!

Cards held behind back

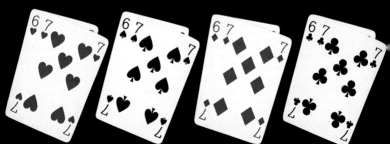

Matching Pairs

Here you predict when a volunteer will tell you to stop dealing. Before you start, secretly put a black nine on the top of the pack and a red three on the bottom.

1. Explain that you will match the cards chosen by a volunteer when he stops you dealing. Look through the pack and take out the other red three and black nine. Lay them face-down, in that order, without showing them.

2. Start dealing the cards face-down, asking your volunteer to tell you when to stop. When he does, lay your red three face-up on the dealt cards. Then put the rest of the pack down on top of it.

3. Now pick up the whole pack and start dealing from the top again. Ask the volunteer to stop you once again, and this time put your black nine face-up on top of the dealt cards. Put the rest of the pack on top.

4. Remind the volunteer that you chose the two cards *before* dealing. Take these out of the pack, with the card above each of them. Reveal the matching pairs.

Some harder tricks

The techniques on the next four pages need quite a lot of practice. But they look very impressive when you can do them smoothly and confidently.

The Glide

The Glide is a sleight of hand which lets you take the next to bottom card from the pack, but which makes it look as if you are taking the bottom card. You may find it easier to do this sleight with new, smooth cards.

1. Pick up the pack face-down with your thumb on one long side and your fingers on the other. Curl your second and third fingers far enough under the pack to get a grip on the bottom card. This is the Glide position.

2. Now do the Glide. As you reach to take a card with your other hand, pull the bottom card back with your second and third fingers. Take the next to bottom card. Then slide the bottom card back into place with your fingers.

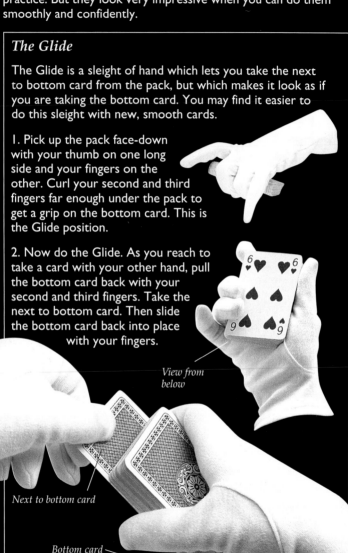

View from below

Next to bottom card

Bottom card

Red and Black

1. Arrange three red and three black cards of any suit and any value in a fan, alternating the reds and blacks. Show them to the audience.

2. Hold the six cards in the Glide position. Take out the bottom card (without doing a Glide). Show it, saying "red", and put it on top of the others.

3. Now take the new bottom card, saying "black". Show it and put it on top of the six cards, as before.

4. For the third card, Glide out the next to bottom card, saying "red". Put it on top of the cards without showing it.

5. Next take the bottom card again, and without showing it to the audience, say "black", and put it on top of the cards.

6. Take the new bottom card, saying "red", and show it to the audience before putting it on top of the other cards.

7. Lastly, do the Glide again and take the next to bottom card. Say "black" and put it on top of the cards without showing it.

8. Deal the cards face-down, saying "black, red, black, red, black, red."

9. Snap your fingers and turn the cards face-up.

The cards have changed order.

Fancy flourishes

In the world of magic, a flourish is a movement designed to catch the audience's attention. Here are two for you to try. Your audience will have more confidence in you if you can handle the cards well.

Kick Cut

Here is a fancy way of cutting the cards, which you can use to impress your audience. With practice, the Kick Cut can be done with one smooth movement.

1. Hold the pack face-down by its shorter edges with your right fingers and thumb.

2. With your right first finger, lift about half the cards off the pack at the top short edge.

3. Swivel the lifted cards to the left, pivoting on your thumb, ready to take them in your left hand.

4. Take the lifted cards with your left hand, then put the cards that are in your right hand on top.

The Riffle Shuffle

This is an impressive way of shuffling cards.

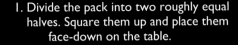

1. Divide the pack into two roughly equal halves. Square them up and place them face-down on the table.

2. Pick up the two halves and rest the bottom outside corners on the table. Position your thumbs on the top inside corners.

3. Push the bottom outside edges down on the table with your hands. Lift the top inside corners of both halves with your thumbs.

4. Now move the two halves together, so the lifted corners overlap. Lift your thumbs slowly, letting cards go. Carry on riffling the pack like this until all the cards have fallen, and the corners of the two halves of the pack are completely interlaced.

5. Now stand the cards on one long edge, interlacing the ends more.

6. Push the halves into each other with your fingers until the pack is squared.

Hold the cards fairly lightly as you push them together.

Index

Note
Be prepared that the tricks on pages 13 and 16-17 may not work if the cards are cut between the Glimpsed card and the chosen card. But don't worry, this is very unlikely.

First published in 1997 by Usborne Publishing Ltd, Usborne House, 83-85 Saffron Hill, London, EC1N 8RT, England.
Copyright © Usborne Publishing Ltd 1997
First published in America August 1997 UE